Just in Time, ABRAHAM LINCOLN

Patricia Polacco

G. P. Putnam's Sons
An Imprint of Penguin Group (USA) Inc.

W hen Michael walked into the double sleeper on the Amtrak Limited bound for Washington, D.C., he said, "This is too cool!"

"Way cool," Derek echoed.

But when the boys were pulling their bedclothes out of their knapsacks, iPods, cell phones and video games tumbled out onto the floor.

"Oh no," their grandmother scolded. "No electronics on this trip—no music, no texting, no tweeting, no e-mailing."

"Then what are we going to do?" the boys howled.

"Do? Well, that's something of a secret, but first stop will be Harpers Ferry, West Virginia, where there is someone I want you both to meet."

Derek slipped his lucky penny from his pocket. "I can keep this, can't I?" he asked.

His grandmother smiled and nodded yes.

The next morning, after they ate breakfast, the train stopped in Harpers Ferry. As it lurched to a stop, a very tall man met them on the platform.

"Mr. Portufoy!" their grandma sang out. "Here are the two grandsons I was telling you about.

"Mr. Portufoy has a marvelous collection of Civil War uniforms, rifles and a wondrous display of the photographs of Mathew Brady and his photographers!"

"Who's Mathew Brady?" Derek asked.

"Aw, everybody knows that. . . . He's the dude that took pictures of battlegrounds during the Civil War." Michael yawned. "We studied him in class."

Mr. Portufoy, their grandma whispered to them, was a "true expert" on the Civil War. The boys looked at each other, bored.

After tea, Mr. Portufoy and their grandmother took the boys to the museum. It was dusty. The Mathew Brady photographs were black and white and definitely boring, one of President Lincoln and some general just standing there.

Then they saw the weapons used in the Civil War—guns and cannons, bayonets and cannonballs.

"Man," Michael exclaimed, running from case to case. "It must have been cool to fight in that war!"

"Way cool," Derek said.

"So you think the Civil War was cool, do you?" Mr. Portufoy mused, and looked at their grandma.

Michael didn't answer. He was eyeing one particularly splendid uniform.

Mr. Portufoy came up behind him. "I have some very authentic uniforms packed away in the archives. Would you like to try one on?"

For the first time since they'd come to Harpers Ferry, the boys smiled. "Would we!" Derek said.

In the archive room, Mr. Portufoy opened an old chest and set out two blue uniforms. "Do you boys know which side used these uniforms?"

"Union!" Michael shouted out. From his history class he knew that the war had been fought between the North and the South because they couldn't agree on slavery. He knew Northern soldiers wore blue, Southern soldiers—called Confederates—wore gray.

Mr. Portufoy began buttoning up the uniform on Derek. "And did you know that President Abraham Lincoln came right here to Harpers Ferry on his way to Antietam?"

"What's Antietam?" Michael asked. He knew about Abraham Lincoln.

"Antietam was one of the most unforgettable battles of the Civil War."

"Hey, I had a video game about the battle of Gettysburg," Derek chirped. "I blew away four hundred soldiers all by myself. I think I set a record."

"Well," Mr. Portufoy said thoughtfully, "how would you like to play something better than a video game? A real game. One that might even take courage!"

"Can we keep the uniforms on?" Michael asked.

"Oh, yes. You *have* to keep the uniforms on . . . that's part of the game."

"Do we get swords and guns?" Derek asked excitedly.

"No swords or guns."

"We don't get to shoot anyone?" Michael whined.

Mr. Portufoy stooped down and took the boys' shoulders. "You are going to Antietam just after the battle. You are going to eat what soldiers eat, walk where they walk, see what they see." Then he looked up at a giant wooden door. "When you walk through that door, you will be in the middle of the . . . game."

He took something gold out of his pocket. "I'm giving you this pocket watch, Michael. Guard this with your life. When you hear the watch chime, you have one hour to get back to this door before sunset. One rule: You cannot tell any of the other players who you really are, nor anything about your modern life. You are young soldiers and it is 1862."

The boys nodded a cautious yes, and Mr. Portufoy nudged them through the door. Their grandmother was nowhere in sight.

On the other side, they were standing right next to their hotel . . . but it was dark. "Whoa," said Derek. "The sun was shining, it was almost lunchtime. Now it's night!"

"Look, Derek," Michael whispered. "No cars. No electric lights, only torchlights."

A small horse-drawn wagon came trotting up and stopped right next to them. "Where've you two been?" an angry voice called out at them. "I've been waiting for you for well nigh an hour!" The boys climbed in and realized they were piled in with stacks of glass photographers' plates and a great big standing camera.

"Derek, that's Mathew Brady!" Michael whispered even though he knew this was just a game.

They stopped in front of a shop that read Photographic Studio. There was already a carriage and a group of soldiers waiting.

"Collect the equipment," the photographer barked. "Load it into the carriage."

But when they came into the store, there was a very tall man in a cape and a tall hat. When he removed his hat, the boys gasped.

"Michael," Derek whispered, "where did they get someone who looks so much like Abraham Lincoln?"

"Mr. President," Mr. Brady said, as he gave him a slight bow. "An honor."

"Mr. Brady, sir, your reputation precedes you. I understand that one of your photographers will photograph my meeting with General McClellan, celebrating the Northern victory at Antietam."

"One of the best, sir."

Wow! Michael thought. What a game!

In the carriage, as it jiggled along, two soldiers sent by General McClellan gave the boys small packets they called "jerky." "It's the last you'll have for some time, boy," one said. Michael thought it tasted like shoe leather.

Then, the two soldiers got to whispering about the battle. How it lasted one day. How thousands of soldiers clashed in a cornfield. How the Northerners met Confederates posted along a sunken road the two soldiers were calling "Bloody Lane."

"Course, it weren't called that until two days ago," one trooper said, his voice breaking.

The other soldier's eyes began to tear. "Those boys walked across that cornfield as if they were invincible. But they weren't."

These soldiers sure talked real. Michael could feel his heart beating through his uniform. Good thing it was just a game.

Mr. Lincoln said not a word. By daybreak they rolled into the encampment at Antietam. When Lincoln climbed out, he chucked Derek under the chin. "I been watching you, boy. You remind me greatly of my boy, Willie." He turned and followed the two troopers.

"Whoever this guy is, he's really good," Derek said.

"You there, boys!" It was the Brady photographer. Already here. He grabbed a camera out of the carriage.

"Alexander Gardner's the name!" he barked. "We gotta use this morning sun." The boys hustled after him across a pasture. A battlefield?

The pattern was always the same: first, by foot, Gardner would search for the picture he wanted, then he'd call for his camera, set the picture up, take it, and move on. He photographed a field of broken cornstalks littered with torn blue caps. He photographed a tree, whose branches were exploded away.

"Here, boy," he'd shout, and Derek or Michael would run to hand him another glass plate. But where were the soldiers, Confederate or Union? What kind of game was this? They said the battle had been over for two days; did the soldiers just go home when the game was over?

But then the photographer moaned, "Oh, my God! Over here." Through a small woods, he'd come upon a low hill with a shed on it. Then Michael saw what the photographer saw: Behind the shed were three soldiers, one sitting, one on his side as if he were swimming, stiff and not moving. Two wore blue, one wore gray.

Beyond them in the distance were more soldiers lying still, as if they were sleeping. And a soldier with a wagon moving around, collecting them.

Michael sat down on the plowed ground, the wind knocked out of him. "Derek," he whispered. "I don't understand it, but this is no game."

"Your first battlefield?" a voice asked sadly. The boys nodded. It was President Lincoln!

He put his hands on their shoulders.

"A terrible thing . . . war." His voice trailed off. "Twenty-three thousand men dead or wounded.

"I can only wonder as I stand here today if it is worth this dreadful sacrifice. . . . My heart breaks that I ordered these lads to their death." He spoke as he walked the boys back to the encampment.

Michael looked at his watch. It was already 3:00! "Derek! The clock hasn't chimed. How can we make it back to Harpers Ferry in time to get through the door by sunset?"

Derek started to cry. "It doesn't matter, Michael. Don't you see—we're here, really here! In the middle of the Civil War. We'll never see Gramma again."

"My dear boys . . . you should have never been out on that battlefield," Mr. Lincoln said as he walked them toward McClellan's tent.

He hugged them both.

"If only I could be assured that all of this death, destruction and loss is worth the price."

Michael could feel the president's heart breaking.

He suddenly knelt in front of him, and it burst out of him. "But Mr. Lincoln, the North is going to win the war. The country will stay together." He caught himself. The game. Mr. Portufoy's one rule. He couldn't tell Mr. Lincoln how he knew!

"If only I could be assured of that, boy," the president whispered. "If only I could be assured that slavery will be abolished and the Union restored, one voice, one country . . . one nation." Mr. Lincoln's eyes seemed as sad as time.

"But it is true, Mr. Lincoln," Derek suddenly sputtered. "We know. We're from the future. You have to believe us! The North is going to win."

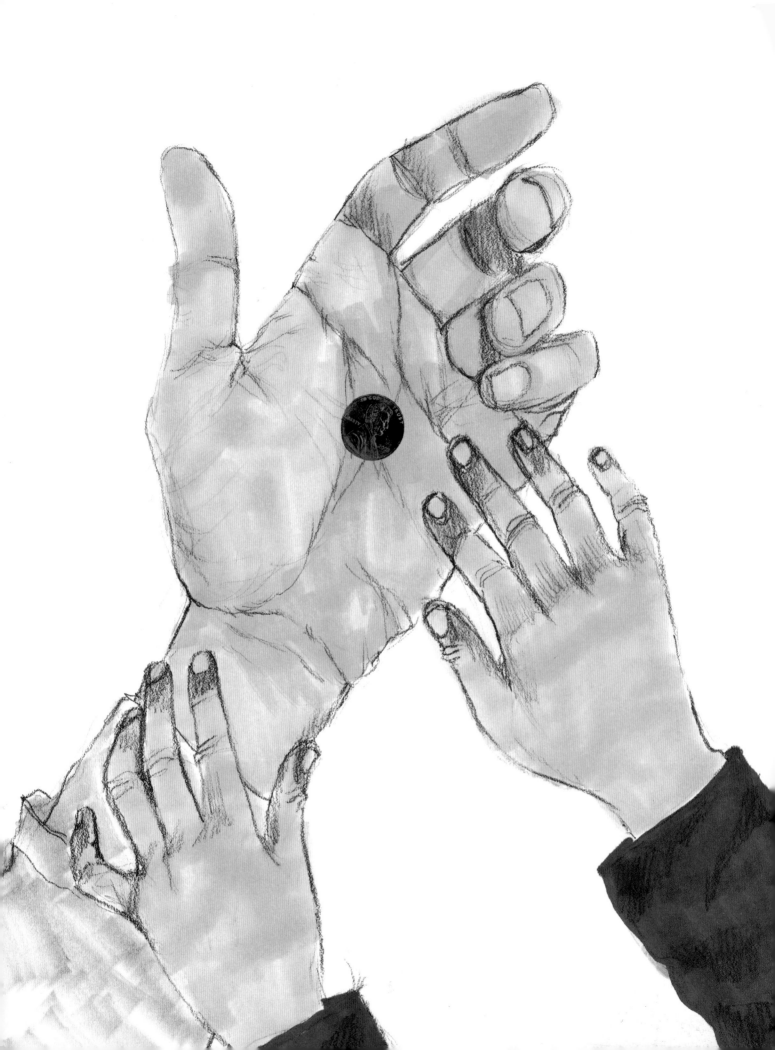

"America will become a powerful nation," Michael whispered, forgetting all about Mr. Portufoy's rules.

"And one day, Mr. Lincoln"—Derek was almost smiling—"a black man will become president!"

"A black man, president!" Mr. Lincoln looked at him, the slightest smile at the corner of his mouth. "A black man president. . . . But where . . . why . . . how are you boys even here at Antietam?"

"It was a game, Mr. Lincoln. Or it was supposed to be, but it wasn't," Derek answered. He started to sob. Mr. Lincoln put his arms around him.

"War is anything but a game, my boy." He was looking straight in Derek's eyes now and took his hand. "I lost my son Will last February from typhoid. A beautiful boy just as you are. I feel that same spirit in you. Foolish, but maybe he sent you to me."

"Wait, Mr. Lincoln. I have proof, my lucky penny—look, it's you . . . look at the date. 2007."

Just then, the photographer Gardner came up behind them. "Look lively, boys, we have to photograph the president and the general . . . the light is just right."

Derek stuffed his lucky penny back into his pocket.

Michael handed glass plate after glass plate to Gardner, then stood back with Derek, as the photographer photographed the general and the president standing. The general and the president sitting.

When he was finished, Gardner bowed. "Thank you, sirs," he said, gathered his equipment and left. President Lincoln walked slowly over to the boys.

The late-afternoon sun was low in the sky; it was getting late. Michael held out

his watch. "When this watch chimes, sir, we have only an hour to get back to Harpers Ferry. But it's so late. We have to leave now."

Without hesitation, Lincoln called one of McClellan's troopers. "These boys need to get back to Harpers Ferry before nightfall. Please advise the general."

Relieved, Michael came up to the president. "Sir, you will go down in history as one of the greatest presidents of the United States that ever lived."

"My, my." Mr. Lincoln smiled warmly at them for a long moment, then he shook both of their hands. "Hurry now, lads. The driver is waiting."

The sun sat on the ridge of pine trees and the horses were galloping along the road when Michael felt the pocket watch finally chime. "We're not going to make it," Derek screamed in panic.

"Sir." Michael leaned into the window. "Is there a faster way to Harpers Ferry?"

"Yes, cross-country!" the soldier shouted back. "May not be safe. Enemy troops."

Michael didn't hesitate. "Let's do it!"

The driver handed back muskets to the boys. "You know how to fire these?"

Derek started to answer no, but Michael nudged him, and they both signaled yes.
"Be on the ready."

For the next while there was no trouble. Then, just as they rounded a bend in the road on a cliff above the Potomac River, they heard war whoops coming from the woods on their right flank.

"All right, Derek, raise your musket, get ready to fire," Michael shouted.

"But, Michael, I can't. I don't know how!" Derek whined.

Then, the coach lurched over and skidded onto its side. The horses broke loose and ran.

The boys were dazed for a time, but when they looked up, on the side of a valley just across the Potomac, they could see little houses nestled. Harpers Ferry!

"We have to run for it! Let's go!"

The boys ran and ran until they could taste blood in the backs of their throats. Finally, they bolted across the rail bridge that leads into Harpers Ferry. Union troops were guarding it, but when they saw the uniforms the boys were wearing, they let them pass.

Finally they ran up the last hill to the door of the museum. But Michael looked at his watch. He sat down in a heap. "It's been more than an hour! We didn't make it, Derek." Michael pulled at the door. Game or not, it was locked. It wouldn't open.

Both boys sat on the doorstep, rocking and crying.

"We're never gonna see Gramma again," Derek sobbed. "We're stuck in 1862—should we have warned Mr. Lincoln about the theater?"

"No, Derek—giving him hope was fine, but if we had told him that, it could have changed history."

At exactly that moment, the door unlatched and squeaked open, spilling the bright lights of the museum onto the alley where they were sitting. They turned.

"You broke the rules," they heard a stern voice say. Mr. Portufoy!

"But some rules are meant to be broken."

At the hotel, the boys ran all the way to their grandmother's room and leapt into her arms.

"You boys act like you haven't seen me in ages. You've only been gone an hour!"

Michael breathed a deep sigh. It had been a game after all. Mr. Lincoln, the battleground, the escape. All of it.

"But Gramma," Derek insisted, "we were really there. At Antietam! We saw dead soldiers, battlefields . . . we saw President Lincoln!"

"Oh, boys, what you took part in was a Reenactment. Entire groups all around the country put on uniforms and act out important battles of the war," their grandmother reassured them.

"No, Gramma, we were there," Derek said.

Their grandmother thought for a time.

"Well, boys, if whatever you experienced made history come to life for you, then that is all that counts!" she crowed.

That afternoon after tea in the museum, the two boys went over to the Civil War photos. There it was, the one by Alexander Gardner: President Lincoln and General McClellan standing in front of the tent.

Michael paused, because there in the background, almost in the shadows, were two boys.

"Gramma . . . come look!" the boys gasped.

Their grandmother came over to the photo.

She adjusted her glasses, her eyes widened, she reeled back.

For there on that wall in the Civil War photo, very clearly, were Michael and Derek.

MY DEAR READERS,

At the Battle at Antietam, September 17, 1862, the Union and Confederate armies together suffered the greatest losses for one day of any Civil War battle—23,000 dead and wounded.

It was a battle General Robert E. Lee could have won. But he didn't, all because of a paper wrapped around three cigars! Just weeks before Antietam, Lee had stood up to the Union army at the Second Battle of Bull Run. Now his goal was to move west and encounter the Union army in the North itself—Maryland! The South was running short of supplies, fall was coming on; if Lee could defeat the Union soldiers in the North, he could raid Northern farms and get much-needed food supplies. Indeed, such a victory would mean a real turning point to the whole war.

But a Union soldier discovered the cigars, opening up the paper covering them to discover that it showed where Lee planned to station his troops at Antietam. The soldier rushed the information to General George McClellan, and this crucial information gave McClellan and the Union army extraordinary advantage.

The actual one-day battle occurred near the village of Sharpsburg at Antietam Creek. A sunken road where the Confederates got trapped became Bloody Lane. A major battleground, one that I have pictured, was a simple cornfield, which in the days that followed became forever after The Cornfield.

My story telescopes time. No one really won the battle at Antietam conclusively. General Lee sent his entire Army of Northern Virginia into action—38,000 soldiers, and even though General McClellan had the cigar-paper information about Lee's plans, McClellan cautiously only sent two thirds of his army into the battle—60,000. It was not enough for a total victory. McClellan would lose his position as commander in chief for this decision. But not for another three months. The actual day that Lincoln visited McClellan and the battlefield was October 3, nearly two weeks after the battle. The two armies would have gathered their wounded and their dead long before that.

Perhaps this story, then, was indeed a reenactment where time can be telescoped, as the grandmother of Derek and Michael said. Or perhaps it was a game like no other, where the magnitude of the moment transcended time itself.

What is true is that the Union won the battle strategically, and this "win" enabled the president shortly after the battle to issue a preliminary Emancipation Proclamation freeing the slaves, and a formal proclamation January 1, 1863, changing the course of history.

Respectfully,

Patricia Polacco

a note from the musicians

The stories of Margaret Wise Brown were read to us as children. We read them to *our* children. So it was with familiarity and fondness that we began this project of creating a soundscape to accompany her poetry.

These unpublished works are so rich in imagery that they invite instrumentation and melodies. Margaret Wise Brown often used simple, spare images that enable a listener to home in on little details—a bell, a bug, a buoy— with an almost meditative focus. "The Mouse's Prayer" and "Sounds in the Night" evoke stillness and quiet so effectively that readers may well imagine being able to hear the far away sounds mentioned in the poems. But her words also invite us into a surprising world of wildness, wandering, and risk taking, where monkeys throw coconuts at the sky and baboons and bears take an outlandish trip to the moon in a hot air balloon.

The mandolin helped us convey the excitement and adventure of "The Noon Balloon" and "When the Man in the Moon Was a Little Boy." We chose to use a thumb piano, a high-strung electric guitar, and a lilting slide guitar to approximate an African sound in "Mambian Melody." The sleepy slide trombone mimics yawning in "Sleep like a Rabbit." In "The Secret Song," long notes from a bass harmonica create a foghorn effect. These sounds fell into place as we sought to mirror the lovely and lively images in Margaret Wise Brown's poetry. We hope you enjoy them!

—Tom Proutt & Emily Gary

Goodnight Songs

by Margaret Wise Brown

Illustrated by Twelve Award-Winning Picture Book Artists

STERLING CHILDREN'S BOOKS

New York

STERLING CHILDREN'S BOOKS
New York

An Imprint of Sterling Publishing Co., Inc.
1166 Avenue of the Americas
New York, NY 10036

Text and lyrics © 2014 Hollins University
Music © 2014 Proutt and Gary

This special edition was printed for Kohl's Department Stores, Inc. (for distribution on behalf of
Kohl's Cares, LLC, its wholly owned subsidiary) by Sterling Publishing Co., Inc.

ISBN 978-1-4549-2893-5

Library of Congress Cataloging-in-Publication Data

Brown, Margaret Wise, 1910-1952.
  Goodnight songs : illustrated by twelve award-winning picture book artists / Margaret Wise Brown.
      pages cm
  Summary: A previously unpublished collection of twelve lullabies, illustrated by contemporary,
award-winning artists including Jonathan Bean, Sophie Blackall, Renata Liwska, and Dan Yaccarino.
  ISBN 978-1-4549-0446-5
  1. Lullabies. 2. Children's songs. [1. Lullabies. 2. Songs.] I. Title.
  PZ8.3.B815Gp 2014
  782.42--dc23
  [E]

                                        2013037539

KOHL'S
Style # 9781454928935
Factory Number: 123386
10/17

For information about custom editions, special sales, and premium and corporate purchases,
please contact Sterling Special Sales at 800-805-5489 or specialsales@sterlingpublishing.com.

Manufactured in China

Lot #:
2   4   6   8   10   9   7   5   3   1
10/17

sterlingpublishing.com

Art Direction and Design by Merideth Harte

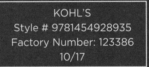

Cover illustration by Melissa Sweet

Illustration for "The Mouse's Prayer" © 2014 by Jonathan Bean; Illustration for "When I Close My Eyes at Night" © 2014 by Carin Berger;
Illustration for "Mambian Melody" © 2014 by Sophie Blackall; Illustration for "Goat on the Mountain" © 2014 by Linda Bleck; Illustrations for title page,
CD envelope, and "The Noon Balloon" © 2014 by Renata Liwska; Illustration for "Wooden Town" © 2014 by Christopher Silas Neal; Illustration for
"Little Donkey Close Your Eyes" © 2014 by Zachariah OHora; Illustration for "Song of Estyn" © 2014 by Eric Puybaret; Illustration for "When the Man
in the Moon Was a Little Boy" © 2014 by Sean Qualls; Illustrations for jacket, CD label, and "Sleep like a Rabbit" © 2014 by Isabel Roxas;
Illustration for "The Secret Song" © 2014 by Melissa Sweet; Illustration for "Sounds in the Night" © 2014 by Dan Yaccarino

introduction

Twenty years ago I found the treasure of a lifetime: hundreds of pages of unpublished manuscripts, poem fragments, and lyrics for songs by Margaret Wise Brown, the bestselling author of *Goodnight Moon*, *The Runaway Bunny*, and so many others. At the time of the discovery I owned a small publishing company that specialized in reprinting vintage children's books, and Margaret was one of the authors whose books I adored. She was universally recognized as one of the foremost authors of children's literature—a prolific writer who dreamed stories at night and hurried to write them down in the morning before she forgot them. No single publisher could keep up with her output, so she created a variety of pen names for her six publishers. When she died unexpectedly at the age of forty-two after a routine appendectomy, the flow of books didn't trickle away; it simply stopped.

While visiting Margaret's sister, Roberta Rauch, on her farm in Vermont, I followed a hunch and asked her if she knew of any unpublished manuscripts. "Oh, yes," was her quick reply. "They're in a trunk in the attic of my barn."

It took months of cajoling to get Roberta to bring down the trunk for me to look through, but when she did, I was astonished. The cedar trunk was filled side-to-side with papers, mostly onionskin pages gathered with rusted paper clips. At first I thought it couldn't possibly be true that the hundreds of typewritten pages had never been published. But as I pored over them during the next two days, I knew these were not stories or poems I had read before. And the handwritten notes scrawled in the margins and between the lines immediately identified the work as Margaret's. The trunk also contained musical scores of Margaret's words put to music. Her sister explained to me that near the end of her life Margaret had become focused on writing songs for children. As she listened to children go about their lives, she realized that they made up songs about whatever it was they were doing at the time. She wanted to capture that spirit of a child's world in her songs the way she had in stories. She thought if she could do that, perhaps children could retain that ability to express their thoughts in song, something that seems to disappear as we grow older.

During what turned out to be her last year, Margaret traveled to France on a book tour. She was under contract to create songs for a new children's record company, and was creating radio and TV shows featuring children's music and stories. Her collaborators were some of the best-known singers and songwriters of her day, including Burl Ives and Rosemary Clooney. While in France, Margaret finalized a manuscript for a poetry collection called *The Green Wind*. Many of the works within *Goodnight Songs* are part of that larger collection. Except for three, "Little Donkey Close Your Eyes," "The Mouse's Prayer," and "The Secret Song," the poems in *Goodnight Songs* have never appeared in print.

Margaret once said that the author of a book didn't seem important to her as a child; it was the story that mattered. Clearly she kept that in mind as she mused about writing: "One can but hope to make a child laugh or feel clear and happy-headed as he follows the simple rhythm to its logical end. It can jog him with the unexpected and comfort him with the familiar, lift him for a few minutes from his own problems of shoelaces that won't tie, and busy parents and mysterious clock time, into the world of a bug or a bear or a bee or a boy living in the timeless world of a story."

Goodnight Songs invites children and their parents into that very world. I am certain that Margaret would be thrilled to see that her words have been brought to life so beautifully through music and illustration.

—*Amy Gary*,
Editor of the Margaret Wise Brown Estate

the noon balloon

The Noon Balloon
Will be leaving soon
For the sun or the moon.
And wherever it goes,
It will get there too soon.

Aboard was a bear
And a crazy baboon
In the Noon Balloon.
And a monkey, a troll,
And a tiny little mole
On a trip to the moon.

And to lands far away
From Every Day,
Where they could arrive
But never stay
For long.

So the Noon Balloon
Is returning soon
From the sun or the moon.
And whenever it comes,
It will get here too soon.

And to lands far away
From Every Day,
Where they could arrive
But never stay
For long.

So the Noon Balloon
Is returning soon
From the sun or the moon.
And whenever it comes,
It will get here too soon.

Mambian Melody

Hum me a Mambian melody,
Soft as the song of a sleepy bee
In a cloudy pink apple tree.
Hum me a Mambian melody.

Hum me a Mambian melody,
Clear to the ear of love, so dear,
Clear as stars by which sailors steer
On a windy Mambian mountainous sea.
Hum me a Mambian melody.

Hum me a Mambian melody,
Soft as the song of a sleepy bee
In a cloudy pink apple tree.
Hum me a Mambian melody.

Hum me a Mambian melody,
Clear to the ear of love, so dear,
Clear as stars by which sailors steer
On a windy Mambian mountainous sea.

Hum me a Mambian melody.

Goat on the Mountain

A goat on the mountain, a goat on the hill
Drank his little supper and drank his fill.
And the goat on the mountain and the goat on the hill
Went to sleep and the night was still.
The stars shone down from the mountain and the hill.

A goat on the mountain, a goat on the hill
Drank his little supper and drank his fill.
And the goat on the mountain and the goat on the hill
Went to sleep and the night was still.
The stars shone down from the mountain and the hill.

Sleep like a Rabbit

Sleep like a rabbit, sleep like a bear.
Sleep like the old cat under the chair.
Sleep like a rabbit, sleep like a bear.
Sleep like the old cat under the chair.

Tuck in your paws and lower your head.
Close your blinking eyes so red.
Take a deep breath on your rabbit bed
And now lie down.

Sleep like a polar bear asleep in the sea,
Flat on his back afloat in the sea,
Up on the waves like a boat in the sea,
Snoozing away like a bear on the sea.

Sleep like a rabbit, sleep like a bear.
Sleep like the old cat under the chair.
Sleep like a rabbit, sleep like a bear.
Sleep like the old cat under the chair.

Why so sleepy little mole,
Curled and tightly sleeping?
There is no noise beneath the ground
And no worms sing.

Little squirrel up in a tree,
Resting there so sleepily,
Fluffy tail about your head
In your little wind-rocked bed.
Curl up there so sleepy.

Sleep like a rabbit, sleep like a bear.
Sleep like the old cat under the chair.
Sleep like a rabbit, sleep like a bear.
Sleep like the old cat under the chair.

WHEN THE MAN IN THE MOON WAS A LITTLE BOY

When the man in the moon was a little boy,
Sing hi ho, the man in the moon,
He ran away with a shooting star.
Ho hum, the man in the moon.

And pretty soon in the dark of the moon
And the sky was lit with an amber light
And all the stars began to fight
By blinking at each other.

When the man in the moon was a little boy,
Sing hi ho, the man in the moon,
He ran away with a shooting star.
Ho hum, the man in the moon.

And they winked
And they blinked
In the enormous night
Till the sun came up
And drove them out of sight
And all the stars began to fight
By blinking at each other.

When the man in the moon was a little boy,
Sing hi ho, the man in the moon.

Song to Estyn

Baby, sail the seven seas
Safely in my arms.
When the waves go up and down,
You are safe from harm.

While the breezes gently blow,
You rock to and fro.
When the gale blows from the south,
You will sail and go.

Baby, sail the seven seas
Safely in my arms.
When the waves go up and down,
You are safe from harm.

When the ocean's white with spray,
You will sail away
Until the rising sun
Ends the voyage just begun.

Baby, sail the seven seas
Safely in my arms.
When the waves go up and down,
You are safe from harm.

While the breezes gently blow,
You rock to and fro.
When the gale blows from the south,
You will sail and go.

Baby, sail the seven seas
Safely in my arms.
When the waves go up and down,
You are safe from harm.

When the ocean's white with spray,
You will sail away
Until the rising sun
Ends the voyage just begun.

THE SECRET SONG

Who saw the petals
Drop from the rose?
"I," said the spider.
"But nobody knows."

Who saw the sunset
Flash on a bird?
"I," said the fish.
"But nobody heard."

Who saw the fog
Come over the sea?
"I," said the sea pigeon.
"Only me."

Who saw the first green light
Of the sun?
"I," said the night owl.
"The only one."

Who saw the moss
Creep over the stone?
"I," said the gray fox.
"All alone."

Who saw the fog
Come over the sea?
"I," said the sea pigeon.
"Only me."

WOODEN TOWN

In the wooden town,
In the wooden town,
The streets ran up
And the streets ran down.
And there wasn't a sound,
There was no one around,
In the late night hour
In the wooden town.

In the wooden town,
In the wooden town,
The streets ran up
And the streets ran down.
And there wasn't a sound,
There was no one around,
In the late night hour
In the wooden town.

In the wooden town,
The streets ran up
And the streets ran down.
And there wasn't a sound
In the late night hour
In the wooden town.

In the wooden town,
There wasn't a sound.
In the wooden town,
There wasn't a sound.

In the wooden town,
The streets ran up
And the streets ran down.
And there wasn't a sound
In the late night hour
In the wooden town,
In the wooden town,
In the wooden town,
In the wooden town.

LITTLE DONKEY CLOSE YOUR EYES

Little Donkey on the hill,
Standing there so very still,
Making faces at the skies.
Little Donkey, close your eyes.

Little Monkey in the tree,
Swinging there so merrily,
Throwing coconuts at the skies.
Little Monkey, close your eyes.

Silly Sheep that slowly crop,
Night has come and you must stop
Chewing grass beneath the skies.
Silly Sheep, now, close your eyes.

Little Pig that squeals about,
Make no noises with your snout.
No more squealing to the skies.
Little Pig, now, close your eyes.

Wild young birds that sweetly sing,
Curve your heads beneath your wing.
Dark night covers all the skies.
Wild young birds, now, close your eyes.

Old black cat down in the barn
Keeping five small kittens warm,
Let the wind blow in the skies.
Dear old black cat, close your eyes.

Little child all tucked in bed
Looking such a sleepy head,
Stars are quiet in the skies.
Little child, now, close your eyes.

When I Close My Eyes at Night

When I close my eyes at night,
In the darkness I see light,
Blue clouds in a big white sky.

When I close my eyes at night,
In the darkness I see light,
Where bright green birds go flying by.

When I close my eyes at night,
In the darkness I see light,
Blue clouds in a big white sky.

When I close my eyes at night,
In the darkness I see light,
Bright green birds go flying by.

Sounds in
the Night

They come softly at first
As cars go by,
As boats whistle
Far away, as dogs bark,
Far away in the night.
The boats and the whistles
And the wheels on the street
And the things people said
All day.
All far, far away.
And night
And sleep.

The Mouse's Prayer

Close my eyes and go to sleep.
Bugs no more on grass blades creep.
Bugs no more and birds no more,
In the woods will come no more

Dream of a weed growing from a seed,
Quietly, quietly from a seed.
In a garden
A slim green weed,
Quietly, quietly from a seed.

Close my eyes and go to sleep.
Bugs no more on grass blades creep.
Bugs no more and birds no more,
In the woods will come no more.

Dream of a mouse
In a quiet house
Saying his prayers
On the back stairs.
Please, please, please,
He prays for a piece of cheese.

Close my eyes and go to sleep.
Bugs no more on grass blades creep.
Bugs no more and birds no more,
In the woods will come no more.

Close my eyes and go to sleep.
Bugs no more on grass blades creep.
Bugs no more and birds no more,
In the woods will come no more.

JONATHAN BEAN earned an MFA from the School of Visual Arts and then dove right into the world of picture book illustration. His first two picture books, *At Night* and *Building Our House*, each won a *Boston Globe-Horn Book* Award. He is also the illustrator of two acclaimed picture books by Lauren Thompson, *The Apple Pie That Papa Baked*, which won the Ezra Jack Keats Award, and *One Starry Night*. Jonathan lives and works in Harrisburg, Pennsylvania.

The art for "The Mouse's Prayer" was made with black and white ink drawings, one for each color. The drawings were then scanned digitally, overlaid, and assigned colors in Photoshop.

CARIN BERGER is the award-winning creator of several picture books, including *Forever Friends*, *Ok Go!*, and *The Little Yellow Leaf*, named one of the *New York Times* Ten Best Illustrated Books of 2008. Carin and her family divide their time between New York City and the Berkshires.

"I grew up with the 'great green room' from *Goodnight Moon*. It was almost a tangible space in my mind, and so when I began to illustrate 'When I Close My Eyes at Night' I could almost picture the narrator peering out of the window of that room. I built the illustration as a little 3D stage and photographed it with Porter Gillespie to create a dreamy, not-quite-real atmosphere."

SOPHIE BLACKALL has illustrated more than thirty books for children including the *New York Times* bestselling series Ivy and Bean and the Ezra Jack Keats Award-winning picture book *Ruby's Wish*. Originally from Australia, Sophie now makes her home in Brooklyn. She recently traveled to India with UNICEF and returned with a head full of peacocks, chattering children, moonlit temples, and patterned saris, all of which inspired her painting for "Mambian Melody."

LINDA BLECK is the illustrator of numerous books for young readers, including Margaret Wise Brown's *The Moon Shines Down*, Deb Pilutti's *The City Kid and the Suburb Kid*, winner of Chicago Public Library's Best of the Best Award, and her own *Pepper Goes to School*, winner of a National Parenting Publication Award.

Linda has always been fascinated by the energy and excitement experienced on a full moon's night, when some creatures fall asleep and others are wide awake. Her illustration for "Goat on the Mountain" was inspired by her fond memories of growing up on an orchard. Plus, she has always wanted to draw a hedgehog.

RENATA LIWSKA'S illustrations are often influenced by memories of her childhood. She is the illustrator of the *New York Times* bestsellers *The Quiet Book* and *The Loud Book* by Deborah Underwood, and is the author and illustrator of *Little Panda* and *The Red Wagon*. Originally from Warsaw, Poland, Renata now lives in Calgary with her husband, Mike.

"While visiting NYC, I was sketching in a lovely little cafe in Greenpoint, Brooklyn, when I received an email asking if I would consider creating the illustration for 'The Noon Balloon.' It caught my imagination right away and I had pretty much finished the drawing by the time I left the cafe. I learned later that the author of the poem, Margaret Wise Brown, was born in Greenpoint. It surely was meant to be!"

CHRISTOPHER SILAS NEAL'S first picture book, *Over and Under the Snow* by Kate Messner was praised in the *New York Times* for its "stunning retro-style illustrations," was a 2011 *New York Times* Editor's Choice, and won an E. B. White Honor Award in 2012. Christopher recently directed short animated videos for both Kate Spade and Anthropologie and was awarded a medal from the Society of Illustrators for his work in motion graphics. He lives in Brooklyn and teaches Illustration at Pratt Institute.

"What began as a sketched row of empty houses evolved organically into the finished art for 'Wooden Town,' with the houses stacked up as a road winds through them like a piece of red ribbon. Perhaps after years of being empty, these houses have begun to take on a life of their own."

ZACHARIAH OHORA'S first book, *Stop Snoring, Bernard!*, won the 2011 Founder's Award at the Society of Illustrators and was the PA One Book for 2012. His latest book is called *No Fits, Nilson!* Zachariah lives and works in Narberth, Pennsylvania, with his wife, Lydia, sons Oskar and Theodore, and a fat cat named Teddy.

"I created the illustration for 'Little Donkey Close Your Eyes' in pen and ink, then added colors and textures digitally. I wanted to explore a limited nighttime palette while creating a realistic space where all these animals might co-exist."

ERIC PUYBARET studied illustration at the École Nationale Supérieure des Arts Décoratifs in Paris. Eric is the bestselling illustrator of *Puff, the Magic Dragon* by Peter Yarrow and Lenny Lipton, and *The Night Before Christmas* performed by Peter, Paul and Mary, along with numerous other books published in the United States and in his native France. Eric created the artwork for "Song to Estyn" using acrylic paint on linen.

SEAN QUALLS has illustrated many books for children, including *Giant Steps to Change the World* by Spike Lee and Tonya Lewis-Lee, and *Before John Was a Jazz Giant* by Carole Boston Weatherford, for which Sean received a Coretta Scott King Illustration Honor. Sean draws inspiration from many influences including Black memorabilia, Americana, outsider art, cave paintings, mythology, music, and vintage children's books. He lives in Brooklyn with his wife, illustrator/author Selina Alko, and their two children. While creating the illustration for "When the Man in the Moon Was a Little Boy," Sean listened to a special playlist of moon-themed songs.

ISABEL ROXAS is an illustrator and graphic designer born and raised in the Philippines. Currently she creates picture books, builds tiny sculptures, and designs paper goods in her Brooklyn studio. A whimsical artist, she has a taste for the slightly odd and uncommon, and for tales that go awry. She illustrated *The Case of the Missing Donut* written by Alison McGhee and *Day at the Market* by May Tobias-Papa, which won the Philippine Children's National Book Award in 2010.

"'Sleep like a Rabbit' is such a quiet, drowsy poem that when I was dreaming up ideas for the illustration, I tried to think of the quietest place one could sleep—which brought to mind snow and how it muffles street noises, and also the stillness of ice. I worked with found paper and paint, and enhanced the final piece on the computer."

MELISSA SWEET is the author and illustrator of *Balloons Over Broadway*, which won the Robert F. Sibert Award for the most distinguished informational book for children. Among the nearly 100 other books she has illustrated are *A River of Words* by Jen Bryant, winner of a Caldecott Honor Medal, and *Day is Done*, by Peter Yarrow. She lives in Rockport, Maine.

"The art for 'The Secret Song' was rendered in watercolor, gouache, collage, and pencil on Twinrocker paper. As I started the piece, I took a ferry to a nearby island where Margaret Wise Brown once had a home. She referred to this house in Maine as 'The Only House,' and though I was not sure which white cottage dotting the coast was hers, it seemed fitting that the art for this poem reflect the wildness of the island."

DAN YACCARINO is the author and illustrator of many children's books including *Doug Unplugged*, *Unlovable*, and *The Fantastic Undersea Life of Jacques Cousteau*. He is also the creator and producer of two animated series, the Parents Choice Award-winning *Oswald* and the Emmy-winning *Willa's Wild Life*, as well as the character designer behind the Emmy-winning *The Backyardigans*. His books have won a host of prestigious awards including the *New York Times* Best Illustrated award, an ALA Notable designation, and the Bologna Ragazzi. Dan lives with his family in New York City. The illustration for "Sounds in the Night" was created with brush and ink on vellum, and Photoshop.

credits

Margaret Wise Brown: All lyrics
Emily Gary: Vocals, bass
Tom Proutt: Vocals and all guitars:
   acoustic, classical, electric, high strung
   acoustic, tenor, resonator
Andrew Gabbert: Cello
Jim Gagnon: Penny whistle
Stuart Gunter: Percussion
Mary Gordon Hall: Harmony vocals
Laura Light: Fiddle
John Lloyd: Trombone
Jeff Romano: Harmonica,
   bass harmonica, thumb piano,
   harmony vocals
Andy Thacker: Mandolin

Engineered, mixed, and mastered by
   Jeff Romano
Produced by Tom Proutt and Emily Gary
   www.tomandemilymusic.com

THE NOON BALLOON
Vocals, bass: Emily Gary
Vocals, guitars: Tom Proutt
Harmonica: Jeff Romano
Mandolin: Andy Thacker
Percussion: Stuart Gunter

MAMBIAN MELODY
Vocals, bass: Emily Gary
Vocals, guitars: Tom Proutt
Thumb piano: Jeff Romano
Percussion: Stuart Gunter

GOAT ON THE MOUNTAIN
Vocals, bass: Emily Gary
Guitars: Tom Proutt
Percussion, spoons: Stuart Gunter
Fiddle: Laura Light

SLEEP LIKE A RABBIT
Vocals, bass: Emily Gary
Vocals, guitars: Tom Proutt
Percussion: Stuart Gunter
Trombone: John Lloyd

WHEN THE MAN IN THE MOON WAS A LITTLE BOY
Vocals, bass: Emily Gary
Vocals, guitars: Tom Proutt
Percussion: Stuart Gunter
Mandolin: Andy Thacker

SONG TO ESTYN
Vocals, bass: Emily Gary
Vocals, guitars: Tom Proutt
Percussion: Stuart Gunter
Penny whistle: Jim Gagnon
Cello: Andrew Gabbert

THE SECRET SONG
Vocals, bass: Emily Gary
Vocals, guitars: Tom Proutt
Harmony vocals: Jeff Romano and
   Mary Gordon Hall
Percussion: Stuart Gunter
Harmonica and bass harmonica:
   Jeff Romano

WOODEN TOWN
Vocals, bass: Emily Gary
Vocals, guitars: Tom Proutt
Percussion: Stuart Gunter
Mandolin: Andy Thacker

LITTLE DONKEY CLOSE YOUR EYES
Vocals, bass: Emily Gary
Vocals, guitars: Tom Proutt
Percussion: Stuart Gunter
Mandolin: Andy Thacker

WHEN I CLOSE MY EYES AT NIGHT
Vocals, bass: Emily Gary
Guitar: Tom Proutt
Percussion: Stuart Gunter

SOUNDS IN THE NIGHT
Vocals, bass: Emily Gary
Vocals, guitars: Tom Proutt
Harmony vocals: Mary Gordon Hall
Percussion: Stuart Gunter

THE MOUSE'S PRAYER
Vocals, bass: Emily Gary
Vocals, guitar: Tom Proutt